Manneke Pis is a small bronze statue located near the Grand-Palace in the center of Brussels. Numerous legends surround the statue and its origin, but one thing is certain – "Brussels' Oldest Citizen" is also one of its most popular.

First American Edition 2005 by Kane/Miller Book Publishers, Inc.
La Jolla, California

Originally published in 2004 in Belgium under the title Ik Plas al seen grote jongen
Copyright ©2004 by Uitgeverij Clavis, Amsterdam - Hasselt

Library of Congress Control Number: 2004108549
Printed and bound in Italy

1 2 3 4 5 6 7 8 9 10

ISBN 1-929132-71-9

Marie-Anne Gillet & Isabelle Gilboux

Standing Up

Kane/Miller
BOOK PUBLISHERS

I was very happy sitting on my potty.
I didn't really think about it;
I just sat down like my big sister.
Then, one day, I saw HIM.

Manneke Pis!
The most famous statue in all of Belgium.
He was right in the center of Brussels,
and he was peeing!
He was peeing STANDING UP!
It looked faaaaantastic.

I stood watching him for a long time.
"Why don't you try it too?" he seemed to say.

No more sitting down for me!
I was going to pee like a big boy.
I'd be like Manneke Pis ...
I would pee STANDING UP.

I started practicing as soon as I got home.
(It was a lot harder
 - and a lot messier -
than it looked.)
The first time didn't go very well.

The second time my aim was a little better.
My shoes stayed dry.
Mostly.
But it still wasn't quite right.

I had to be quick the third time.
I had to go bad.
REALLY BAD.
It was a close one.

The fourth time was much better!
It went in the right direction and everything.
Well, almost.

The fifth time I aimed straight ahead.
I thought it was great, but...
The people on the street didn't.

The next time I looked for a quiet spot, someplace where I could be by myself. (Well, almost by myself.)

Soon I could do it almost perfectly.
I practiced everywhere –
in the bathroom,
on the grass,
against a tree,
against the wall –
and soon it worked everywhere, too.

Finally, I was ready.
I was ready to stand up next to my dad.
He looked over and winked at me.
"Now you're a big boy," he seemed to say.
It was terrrrrific!

Sitting on my potty like my big sister was fine.
But I really like standing up!
Just like Manneke Pis.
Just like Daddy.
Plus, I don't have to wait in line.